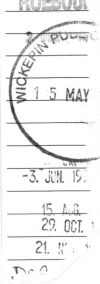

THE 14 FOREST MICE

and the

HARVEST MOON WATCH

By Kazuo Iwamura
English text by MaryLee Knowlton

Gareth Stevens Children's Books
MILWAUKEE

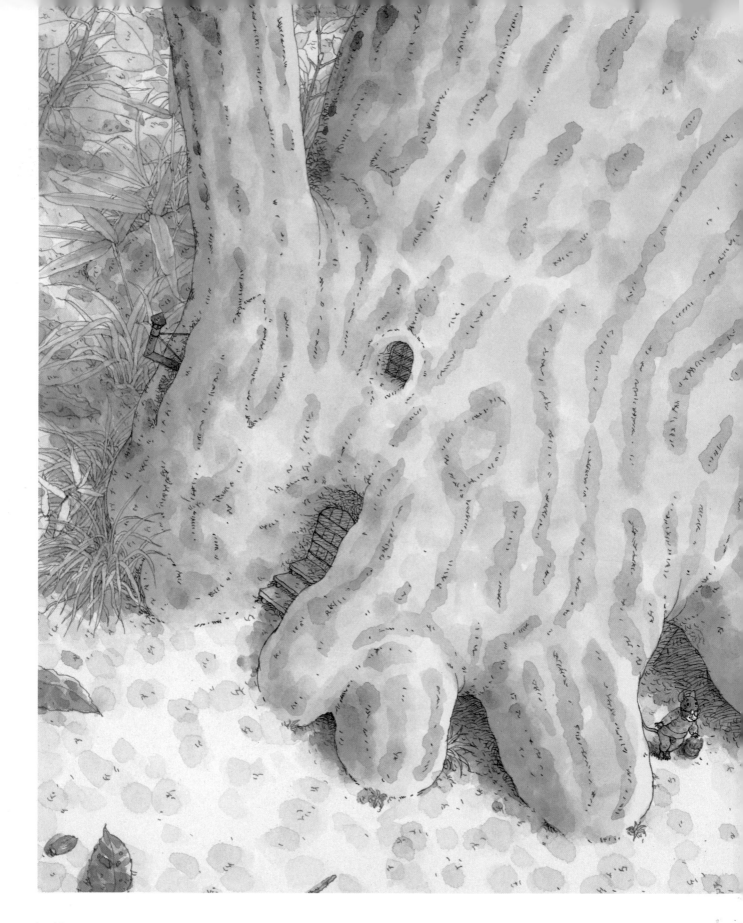

The autumn air was crisp and cool. Only a few leaves had changed color and fallen. Tonight, up in the treetop, the Woodmouse

2

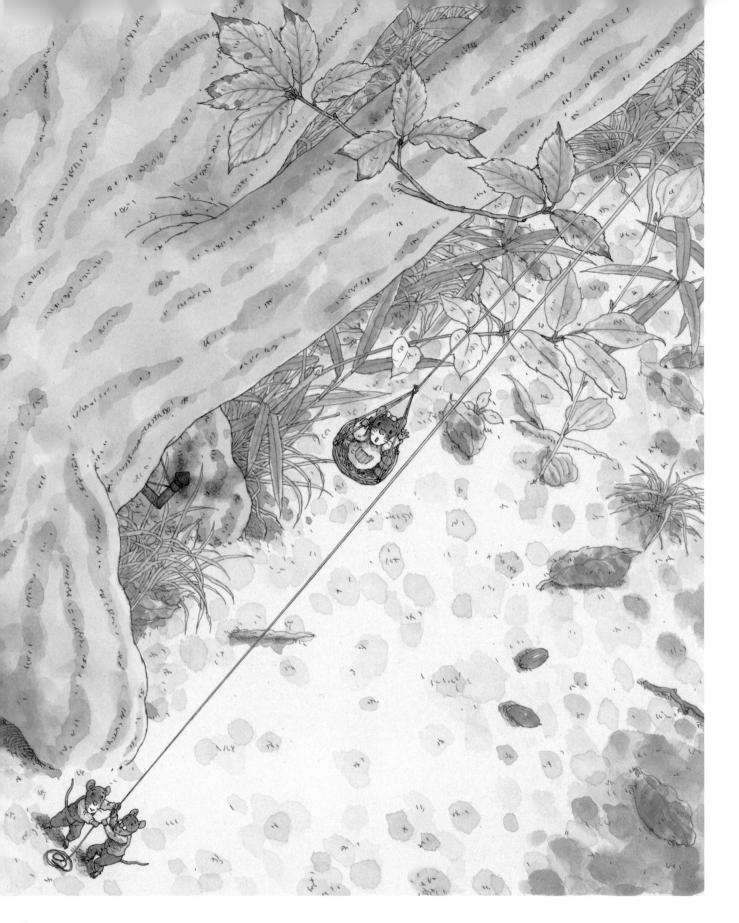

family would be celebrating the harvest moon.
"Here I come!" called out Iris as Papa and
Grandpa hoisted her basket high into the tree.

The first big branch marked the end of the
route for the basket. Daisy and Pecan were

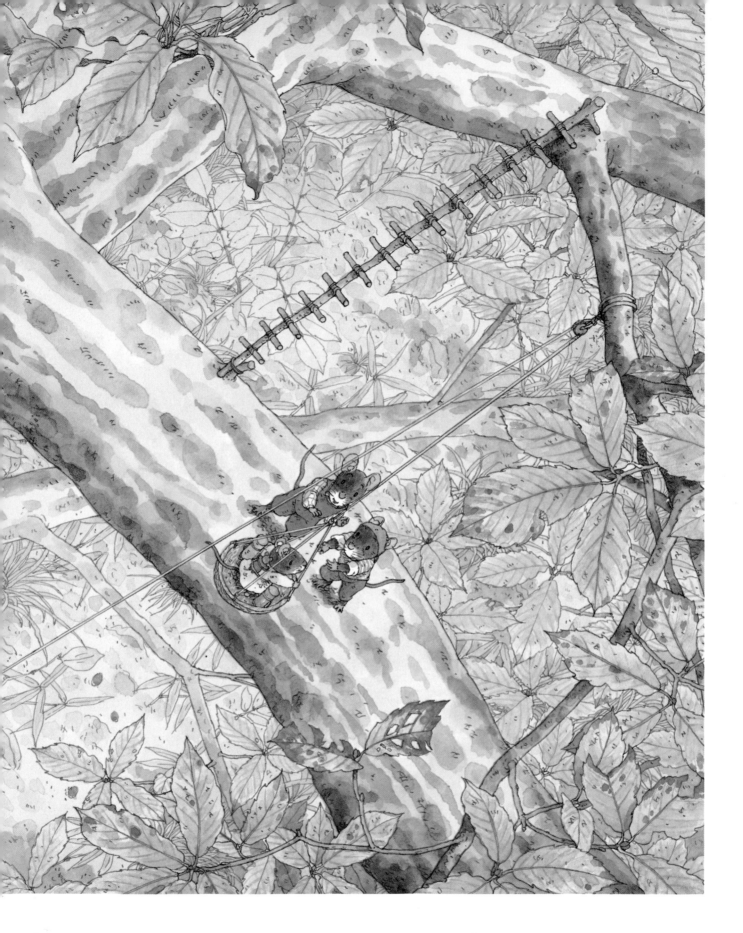

waiting to take their sister the rest of the way.
Now the climb would continue on ladders.

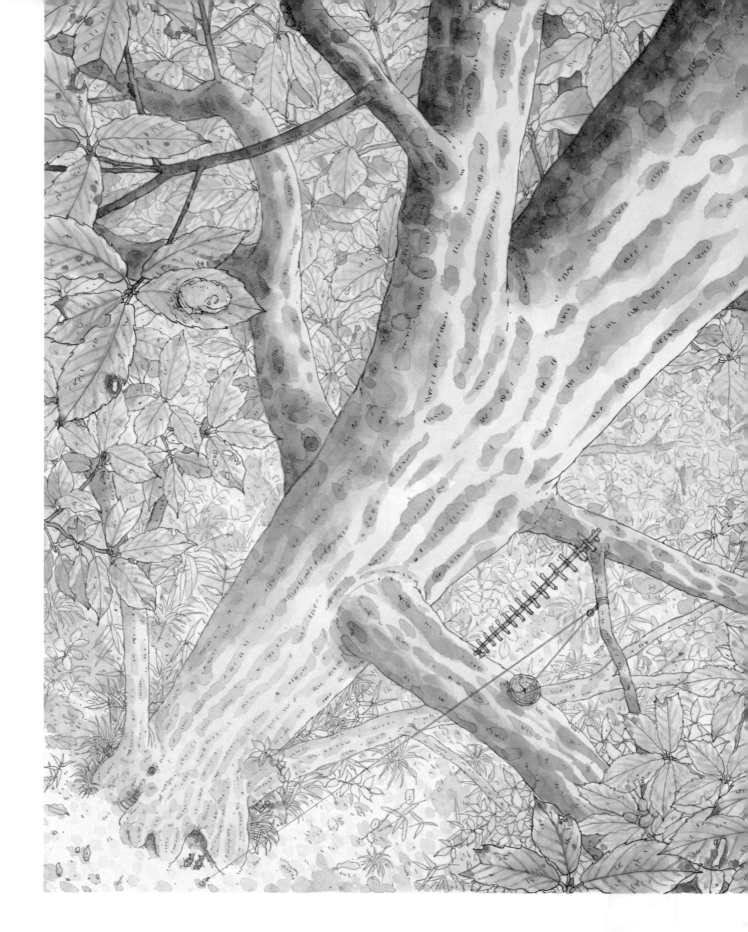

Higher and higher through the tall tree the
three little Woodmice climbed. They passed
an old tree toad napping on a leaf.

6

The leaves rustled softly as the Woodmice
brushed by. "Are we almost there?" little
Iris wondered.

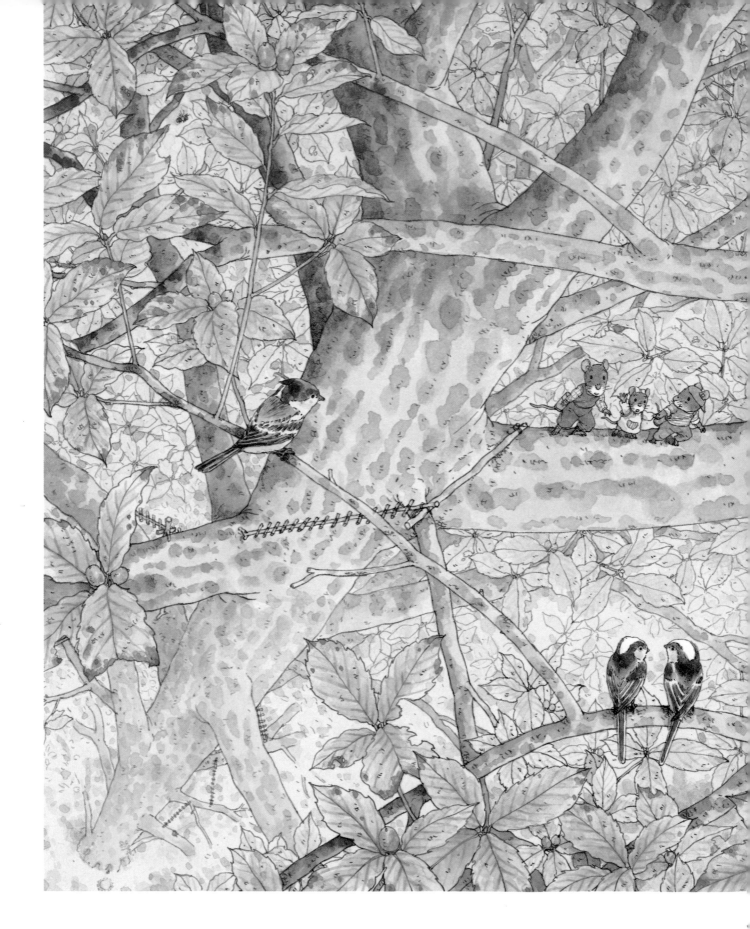

At last the three little Woodmice reached
the treetop! Their busy brothers and sister
welcomed them.

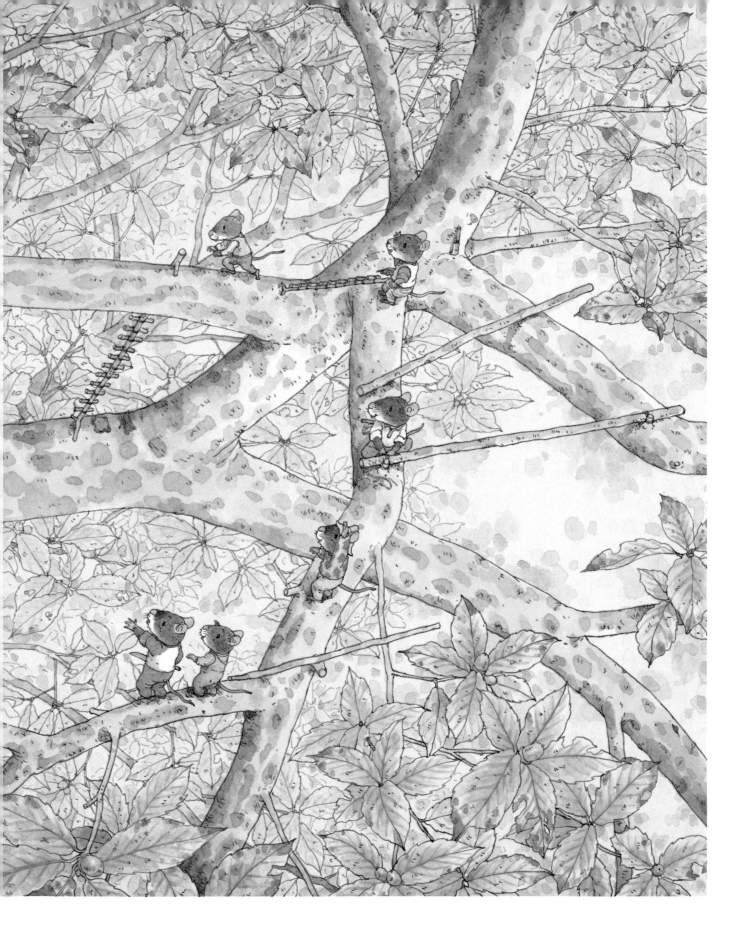

"Help at last!" they cheered. They had
been working since morning and still had
a lot to do.

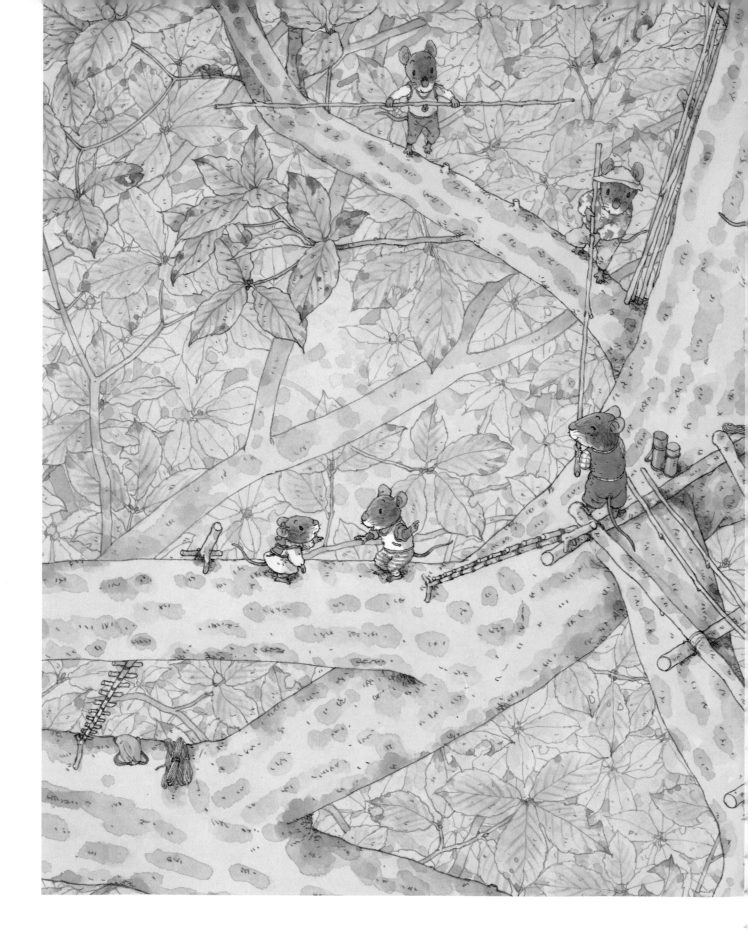

The Woodmice got right back to their work —
cutting and carrying, measuring and fitting!

A ladybug and an inchworm stopped for a look.
What could they be building with those twigs?

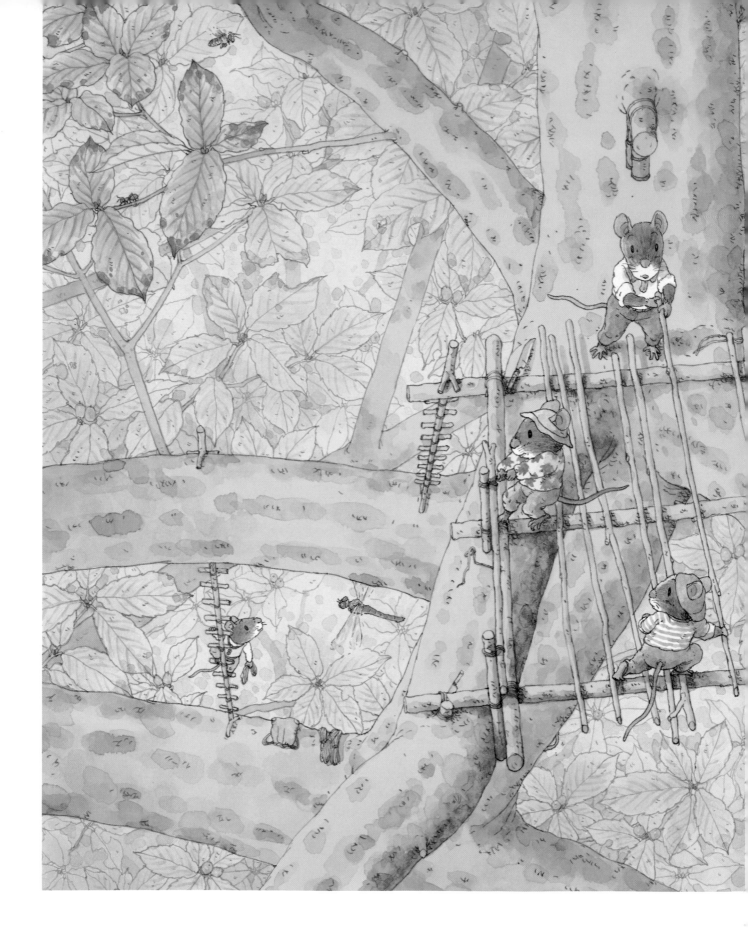

Through the long afternoon, the little
Woodmice toiled. A dragonfly hovered

nearby — a sure sign of a clear night.
Bonk! A nut bounced off Cashew's head.

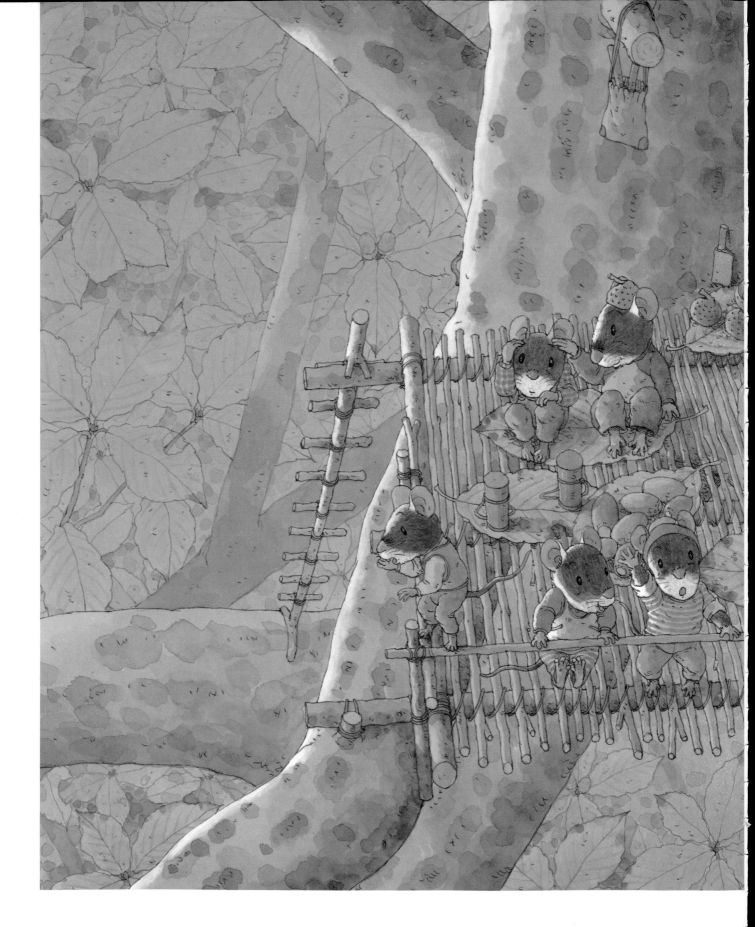

Ah! Finished at last! The little Woodmice
had built a moon-watching platform.
What a wonderful place to celebrate the

14

harvest moon! "Come on up!" Chestnut
called to their parents and grandparents.

The crimson sun of twilight slowly sank
below the horizon. "The harvest moon will

be here soon," said Daisy. The little Woodmice
practiced their patience.

Darkness was settling as the grown-ups arrived carrying the baby and food for a feast.

How thrilled they were to see the platform
the young ones had built!

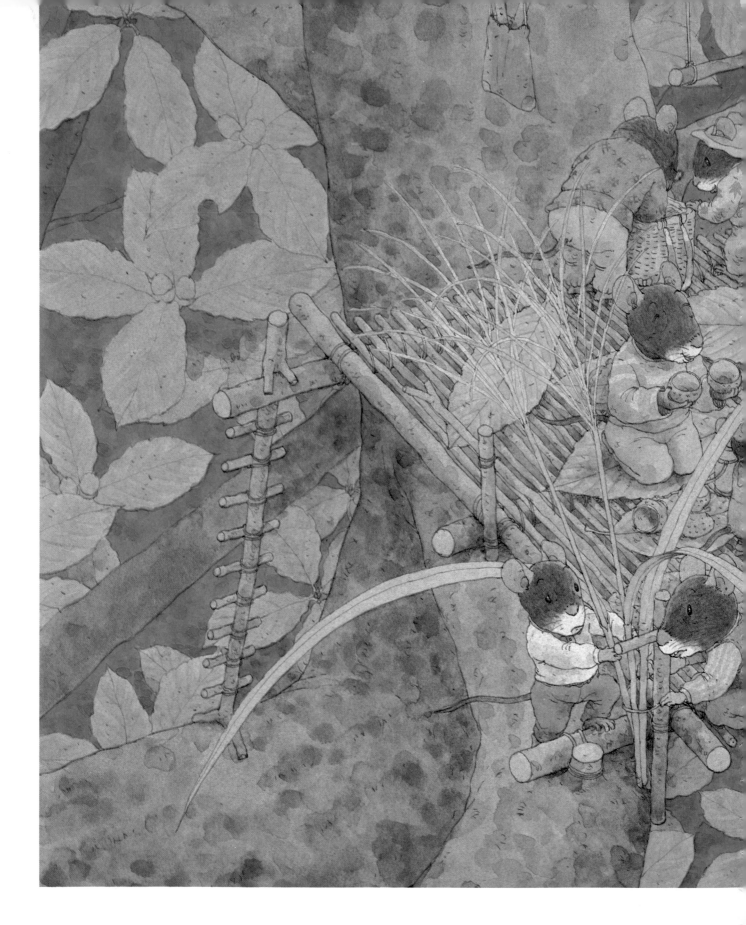

Fresh fall nuts and seeds! Sweet dumplings
and delicious apple juice! What a fine feast

the Woodmouse family would have in the
crisp night air.

There it was! The Woodmouse family
watched in wonder as the harvest moon

climbed over the hill. "How lovely! What magic!" their voices murmured, soft and low.

And now it had risen. The full harvest moon
glided across the night sky.

The little Woodmice had never imagined it
would be so big.

The older Woodmice thanked the moon
for its rich harvest and gentle light.

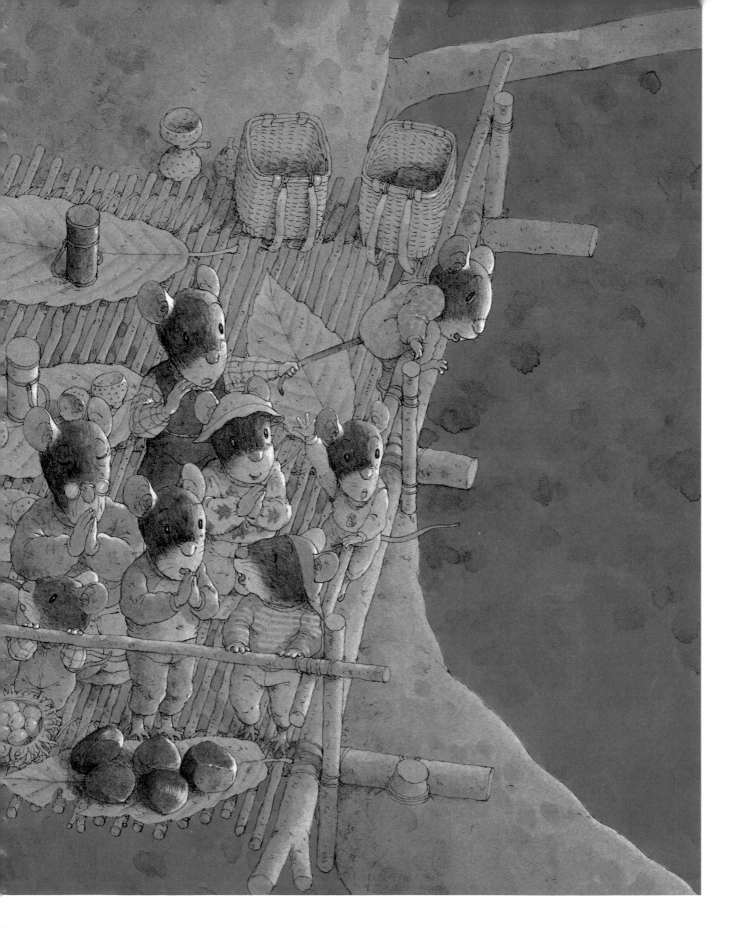

The little ones wondered when it would be
time to eat!

The Woodmice feasted as the harvest moon
rose still higher.

The sounds of sweet music and old stories
floated through the quiet night air.

Soon silence descended on the forest. For hours to come, the night sky would be aglow

with the brilliance of the harvest moon. But
the Woodmouse family was fast asleep.

For a free color catalog describing Gareth Stevens' list of high-quality children's books, call
1-800-341-3569 (USA) or 1-800-461-9120 (Canada).

THE 14 FOREST MICE
THE 14 FOREST MICE and the SPRING MEADOW PICNIC
THE 14 FOREST MICE and the SUMMER LAUNDRY DAY
THE 14 FOREST MICE and the HARVEST MOON WATCH
THE 14 FOREST MICE and the WINTER SLEDDING DAY

Library of Congress Cataloging-in-Publication Data

Iwamura, Kazuo, 1939-
The fourteen forest mice and the harvest moon watch / by Kazuo Iwamura ;
[English text, MaryLee Knowlton]. — North American ed.
p. cm. — (The Fourteen forest mice)
Summary: Members of the Forest Mouse family encounter tree frogs, dragonflies, inchworms,
and birds as they climb a tree to enjoy the beauty of the setting sun and the rising moon.
ISBN 0-8368-0497-X
[1. Mice—Fiction. 2. Nature—Fiction.] I. Knowlton, MaryLee, 1946- . II. Title. III. Title:
14 forest mice and the harvest moon watch. IV. Series: Iwamura, Kazuo, 1939- Fourteen forest mice.
PZ7.I954Fo 1991   [E]—dc20   90-50706

North American edition first published in 1991 by
Gareth Stevens Children's Books
1555 North RiverCenter Drive, Suite 201
Milwaukee, Wisconsin 53212, USA

Design: Kristi Ludwig

Printed in the United States of America

1 2 3 4 5 6 7 8 9 9 97 96 95 94 93 92 91